MINI CLASSICS

GOLDILOCKS
AND THE THREE
BEARS

© Parragon Book Service Ltd

This edition printed for:
Shooting Star Press, Inc.
230 Fifth Avenue–Suite 1212,
New York, NY 10001

Shooting Star Press books are available at special
discounts for bulk purchases for sales promotions,
premiums, fund-raising, or educational use. Special
editions or book excerpts can also be created to
specification. For details contact: Special Sales
Director, Shooting Star Press, Inc., 230 Fifth Avenue,
Suite 1212, New York, New York 10001.

ISBN 1 56924 211 9

Printed and bound in Great Britain.

MINI CLASSICS

GOLDILOCKS
AND THE THREE
BEARS

RETOLD BY STEPHANIE LASLETT
ILLUSTRATED BY NIGEL MCMULLEN

SHOOTING STAR PRESS

Once upon a time there were Three Bears. There was a large, gruff Father Bear, a middle-sized Mother Bear and a little, small, wee Baby Bear.

Father Bear wore baggy
checked trousers held up
with old blue braces.

His tweed jacket had leather patches on the elbows and was a little too tight around the tummy. He loved his food and never left the house without a small snack wrapped up in a red

spotted handkerchief
which he tucked away
inside his cloth cap.

"Just to fill the corners,"
he explained, patting
his round furry stomach.

Mother Bear was plump
and cuddly. She had

dimples in her chubby
cheeks and she winked
her eyes whenever she
laughed, which was often
because she was a very
jolly bear. She wore a
blue and white spotted
dress with a deep frill.

She smelled of currant
buns and warm bread,
especially on baking
day. Then she would
cook tray after tray of
good things to eat, until

the kitchen table could
hold no more and her
face was dotted with
white smudges of flour.

Baby Bear was the
sweetest little bear you
could ever imagine. His
golden fur was as soft as
thistledown. His shining
brown eyes were full of
mischief and his little
button nose was as black

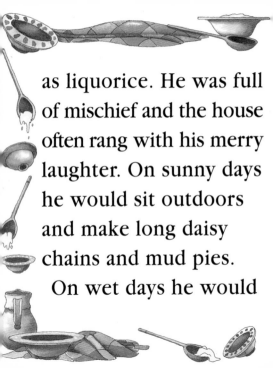

as liquorice. He was full of mischief and the house often rang with his merry laughter. On sunny days he would sit outdoors and make long daisy chains and mud pies.

On wet days he would

snuggle on his mother's lap and watch the raindrops run races down the windowpanes.

The Three Bears lived all together in a little wooden house right in the middle of a forest.

The house was as warm
and as snug as a dormouse
nest. Father Bear was a
very clever carpenter
and had made all the

furniture himself. There
was a fine carved table
and a cupboard for
their bear essentials.

Tucked around the
table were three fine
chairs. There was a
large chair for Father

Bear, a middle-sized chair for Mother Bear and a little, small, wee chair for Baby Bear.

Logs crackled on the open fire and a large pot simmered over the flames. A tall grandfather clock ticked slowly away in a corner of the room and on the hour the chimes rang out and a

little hatch would open
at the top of the casing.
 Out bobbed a brown
honey bee on a bouncing
spring, followed by
three little bears: a
Father Bear, a Mother
Bear and a Baby Bear.

The bears hopped and danced as they chased the bee with outstretched paws — but they never quite caught up and, as the chimes ended, the bee always flew back into the clock ahead of them.

Upstairs were three beds and a wardrobe for their bear necessities. There was a great big bed for Father Bear, a middle-sized bed for Mother Bear and a little, small, wee bed for Baby Bear.

Mother Bear had stitched patchwork quilts for each of the beds and cushions to pile high on the chairs.

Baby Bear had painted bright pictures which they hung on the walls.

Outside in the garden
honey bees buzzed round
the hives and doves
cooed in the dovecot. A
scarebearcrow stood
guard over the vegetables
and tall sunflowers
nodded by the gate.

29

The Three Bears loved
their little home and
thought the forest was a
wonderful place to live.
In the spring, the trees
were bursting with new
buds. Joyful birdsong
was carried on the warm

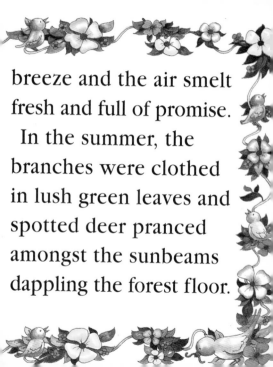

breeze and the air smelt
fresh and full of promise.
In the summer, the
branches were clothed
in lush green leaves and
spotted deer pranced
amongst the sunbeams
dappling the forest floor.

When autumn came the leaves fell — yellow, orange, gold and brown. They gathered in deep drifts and Baby Bear loved to kick through them as he walked through the wood.

In the winter, the bare branches stood stark against a grey sky. Icicles dripped from the eaves of the little house and all the forest sounds were muffled under a deep blanket of snow.

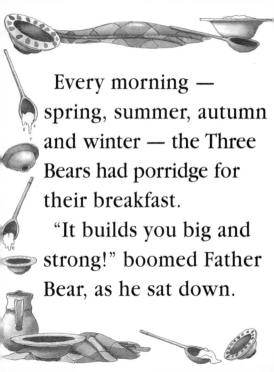

Every morning —
spring, summer, autumn
and winter — the Three
Bears had porridge for
their breakfast.

"It builds you big and
strong!" boomed Father
Bear, as he sat down.

"It warms up your tummy!" smiled Mother Bear, as she tucked in.

"And it tastes yummy!" giggled Baby Bear.

There was a large porridge bowl for Father Bear, a middle-

sized porridge bowl for
Mother Bear and a little,
small, wee porridge
bowl for Baby Bear.

Father Bear's bowl was red with white spots. Mother Bear's bowl was green and painted with yellow marigolds. Baby Bear's bowl was blue and had brown honey pots all around the rim.

One sunny morning
the Three Bears all sat
down together to have
their breakfast but they
found the porridge was
much too hot to eat.

"Let's go for a walk in
the forest while our

porridge cools down," said Father Bear.

Now, while they were out walking, who should come by but a little girl. She had long golden hair and her name was Goldilocks.

"What a sweet little house," said Goldilocks. "I wonder if anyone is at home?"

She looked through the window and peeped through the keyhole but there was no-one to be seen. Goldilocks was a curious little girl so she lifted the door latch and stepped inside.

"Hello," she called. "Is there anybody there?" But all was quiet and still. Then Goldilocks saw the porridge on the table. "Mmmm, that looks good!" she said, licking her lips. Now if Miss

Goldilocks was a polite
little girl she would have
waited until the Bears
came home. Then,
perhaps, they would
have invited her to share
their breakfast, for they
were good Bears.

They were a little rough sometimes, as Bears can be, but for all that very gentle and friendly.

But Goldilocks was a naughty little girl and did not want to wait.

First, she tasted Father Bear's porridge, but that was too hot. Then she tasted Mother Bear's porridge, but that was

too cold. So then she
picked up Baby Bear's
tiny spoon and tasted
his porridge. It wasn't
too hot and it wasn't
too cold. It was just right!
In next to no time Baby
Bear's bowl was empty.

Greedy Goldilocks had
eaten it all up!

Now she felt so full of
porridge that she had to
sit down. First she tried
Father Bear's chair. It
had a flat wooden seat
and a high back made

of thin wooden spindles.
Goldilocks sat down —
but she soon scrambled
off again.

"What a horrid, hard
chair!" she complained.

Then she tried Mother
Bear's chair. It was large

and squishy and filled to
overflowing with fat
feather cushions.

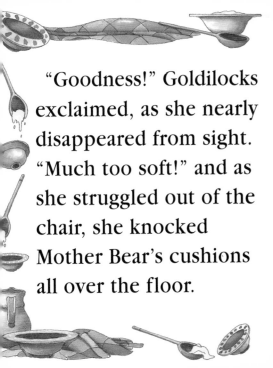

"Goodness!" Goldilocks exclaimed, as she nearly disappeared from sight. "Much too soft!" and as she struggled out of the chair, she knocked Mother Bear's cushions all over the floor.

Then she tried Baby Bear's little rocking chair. Father Bear had carved garden flowers into the oak and hidden amongst them were all the birds of the forest. Goldilocks sat down.

It wasn't too hard and it wasn't too soft. This chair was just right! "Perfect!" sighed Goldilocks, happily.

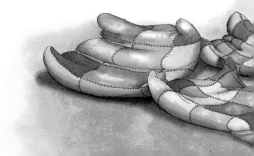

With a tummy full of porridge and a big smile on her face, Goldilocks leant back and made herself comfortable. But she was too big and heavy for Baby Bear's little chair and with a

creak and a crash, it
broke into tiny pieces.
Goldilocks was cross!
"Maybe I can rest
upstairs," she thought
and up the rickety
wooden stairs she went.
The bedroom was tucked

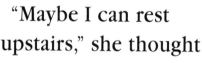

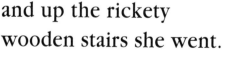

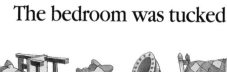

under the rafters in the
roof. It was cosy and
warm and Goldilocks
yawned sleepily as she

looked at the three beds. First she tried to lie down on Father Bear's big bed, but it was so

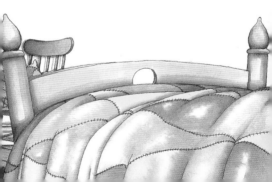

high that she could not
climb up onto it. She
tried to pull herself up
but only succeeded in
pulling the pillow onto
the floor!

"I can't climb up there," she sighed. Then she sat down on Mother Bear's bed. It was soft and squidgy and very, very low down.

"It will feel as if I am sleeping on the floor and I won't like that," complained Goldilocks.

Then she spotted Baby Bear's little bed. It wasn't too high and it wasn't too low. It was just right!

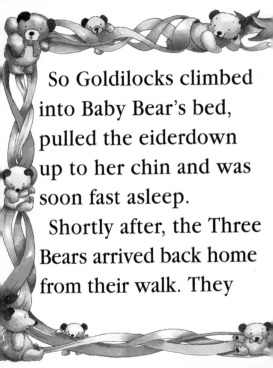

So Goldilocks climbed into Baby Bear's bed, pulled the eiderdown up to her chin and was soon fast asleep.

Shortly after, the Three Bears arrived back home from their walk. They

were all looking forward
to eating their bowls of
porridge and with
rumbling tummies they
sat down at the table to
have their breakfast.
Straightaway they knew
something was wrong.

"Someone's been eating my porridge!" roared Father Bear.

Mother Bear looked at her plate.

"Someone's been eating my porridge!" she growled.

Then the little, small,
wee Baby Bear looked
at his empty plate.

"Someone's been
eating my porridge," he
squeaked, "and they've
eaten it all up!"

The Three Bears looked around them. Then Father Bear noticed that his favourite seat had been moved from its usual position close by the fireside.

"Someone's been sitting

in my chair!" Father
Bear bellowed.

Mother Bear saw that
her soft cushions were
lying all over the floor.

"Someone's been sitting
in my chair!" she grunted.

Then Baby Bear realised

that the wooden splinters
covering the rug were
all that remained of his
favourite little chair.
"Someone's been sitting
in my chair," he wailed,
"and they've broken it
into pieces!"

83

Then the Three Bears
decided to hunt all
through the house until
they found the naughty
person who had visited
them whilst they were
out walking in the forest.
Up the rickety wooden

stairs they all went, thump! thump! thump! Straightaway, Father Bear noticed that the pillow had been pulled off his bed.

"Someone's been sleeping in my bed!" he grumbled.

Then Mother Bear looked closely at her bed and saw that her blanket was crumpled. "Someone's been

sleeping in my bed!"
she rumbled.
 And when Baby Bear
came to look at his bed,
who should he find
tucked up under the
covers but a little girl
with long golden hair!

"Someone's been sleeping in my bed," he squealed, "and she's still there!"

Now Baby Bear's voice was so squeaky and shrill that it woke up Goldilocks at once. And what a fright she had when she saw the Three Bears looking so fierce and cross!

Up she jumped and ran
like the wind down the
rickety wooden stairs.
Out of the door she
flew and she didn't stop
running until she was
far away from the little
house and the Three

Bears. And, after that, they never saw Goldilocks again!

The origin of this story is uncertain but the first printed version of *The Three Bears* appeared in 1837 and was written by the poet, Robert Southey. His story, however, is almost certainly based on a traditional folk tale where instead of Goldilocks, an angry old woman enters the house and samples the porridge!

Over the years the old woman changed into a little girl called Silver-Hair, then Silverlocks and finally ended up as Goldilocks in a new version of the story printed in 1904. The rest of the story has remained exactly the same but nobody has ever seemed quite certain how to give it a satisfactory ending. Some early versions had the old woman taken to a House of Correction by the village constable; one had her thrown "aloft on St Paul's church-yard steeple", but most end with Goldilocks simply running off into the wood, never to be seen again!